MACBETH

GOLD EDITION

WILLIAM SHAKESPEARE

EDITED BY
ADAPTIVE READER

ISBN: 979-8-8692-9735-8

CONTENTS

INTRODUCTION

Welcome to Adaptive Reader, your portal to the captivating world of literature, tailored to fit your unique reading abilities.

In today's fast-paced and diverse learning environment, we believe in the power of personalized learning experiences. That's where the concept of leveled reading comes in, and why we, at Adaptive Reader, have dedicated ourselves to offering a broad collection of classic novels at various reading levels. Our mission is to make the joy and benefits of reading accessible to everyone.

THE BENEFITS OF LEVELED TEXTS

So, what exactly is leveled reading? It's an approach that matches students with texts that align with their unique reading abilities. This ensures that every reader is challenged just the right amount - enough to grow, but not so much that they feel overwhelmed or frustrated.

For students, this means you'll engage with texts that stretch your reading skills while keeping the experience enjoyable and manageable. You'll gain confidence as you successfully comprehend each level and feel motivated to explore more challenging texts as your reading skills grow.

For teachers, Adaptive Reader provides a valuable tool to support differentiated instruction. You can assign the same novel to your entire class while ensuring each student reads a version that aligns with their reading level. This allows all students to participate in class discussions and activities, fostering a more inclusive learning environment.

For parents, Adaptive Reader offers a supportive tool to encourage your children's reading journey. As your child progresses through the different levels of a novel, they'll not only enhance their reading skills but also develop a deeper love for literature.

READING ACROSS MULTIPLE EDITIONS

All of our leveled novels include passage markers that correspond to the same content across every one of our editions. This means that passage '62' in our silver edition contains the same themes and plot elements as passage '62' in our original edition.

For teachers, this means that you can say "let's look at passage 35 together. What is the author trying to tell us here?" and all of your students will be reading the same content — but with vocabulary and syntax that's adapted to their reading level.

Our online reading tool, available at www.adaptivereader.com, gives students and teachers free access to the original text with passage markers. We encourage teachers to include close readings of the original text as part of their coursework, giving all students exposure to the rich original syntax and language of these exceptional authors.

THE POWER OF LITERATURE

At Adaptive Reader, we are committed to helping everyone experience the power of literature. So whether you're a student diving into a classic novel, a teacher looking for flexible resources, or a parent seeking ways to support your child's literacy, Adaptive Reader is here for you.

We invite you to embark on this exciting literary journey with us. Enjoy the world of stories, characters, and ideas that await you in our collection of leveled novels. Happy reading!

DRAMATIS PERSONÆ

DUNCAN: King of Scotland.

MALCOLM: Duncan's older son.

DONALBAIN: Duncan's younger son.

MACBETH: A thane and officer in the King's army.

BANQUO: A thane and officer in the King's army.

MACDUFF: A thane in Scotland, referred to as a Nobleman.

LENNOX: A thane in Scotland, also a Nobleman.

ROSS: A thane in Scotland, also a Nobleman.

MENTEITH, **ANGUS**, and **CAITHNESS**, all of whom are Noblemen of Scotland.

FLEANCE: The son of Banquo.

SIWARD: The Earl of Northumberland and the leader of the English forces.

YOUNG SIWARD: Siward's son.

SEYTON: An officer who supports Macbeth.

YOUNG BOY: Macduff's son.

DOCTOR: attends to the ill.

PORTER: and an elderly doorman.

LADY MACBETH: Macbeth's wife.

LADY MACDUFF: Macduff's wife.

GENTLEWOMAN: takes care of Lady Macbeth, similar to a personal servant.

HECATE, and three mysterious women, known as the Witches.

There are **LORDS, GENTLEMEN, OFFICERS, SOLDIERS, MURDERERS**.

SCENE: The play is primarily set in Scotland and for one scene, in England.

ACT 1

SCENE 1. AN OPEN PLACE

[Thunder and lightning. Enter three witches.]

FIRST WITCH:
When will we gather again?
In thunderstorms, lightning, or during the rain?
SECOND WITCH:
When the noise is done,
When the battle is both lost and won.
THIRD WITCH:
That will be before sunset.
FIRST WITCH:
Where's the meeting spot?
SECOND WITCH:
On the open, wide space.
THIRD WITCH:
There we'll meet with Macbeth.
FIRST WITCH:
I'm on my way, Graymalkin!

SECOND WITCH:
Paddock calls us.
THIRD WITCH:
I'll be there shortly.
ALL:
What's good is bad, what's bad is good:
Float through the misty and filthy air.

Exit.

SCENE II. A CAMP NEAR FORRES

3   *[Alarm sounds within. Enter King Duncan, Malcolm, Donalbain, Lennox, with helpers, meeting a wounded soldier.]*

DUNCAN:

Who is this bloody man? It seems

He can tell us of the recent battle.

MALCOLM:

This is the soldier

Who, like a brave and tough warrior, fought

against my capture.—Hello, friend!

Tell the King what you know about the battle

As you last saw it.

SOLDIER:

It was uncertain;

Like two tired swimmers clinging to each other,

Their own struggle, choking them. The cruel Macdonwald

(He deserves to be called that because of

how evils he is and what

Has come upon him), from the Western Isles
Received support from footsoldiers and others;
And Fortune, smiling on his cursed fight,
Made him seem like a rebel's champion. But it wasn't enough;
For brave Macbeth (he certainly earned that reputation),
Ignoring Fortune, waving his sword,
Still hot with violent action,
Like Courage's favorite, fought his way,
Until he faced the enemy;
Who never greeted Macbeth, nor said goodbye,
Until Macbeth ripped him open from the navel to the jaw,
And mounted his head on our walls.
DUNCAN:
Oh brave cousin! Great soldier!
SOLDIER:
As the sun begins to rise,
Shipwrecking storms and terrible thunder strikes,
So from that source, where comfort seemed to come,
Discomfort grows. Pay attention, King of Scotland:
As soon as justice was had, with strength, equipped itself,
The Norwegian army general, seeing an opportunity,
With new weapons and fresh troops,
Launched a new attack.
DUNCAN:
Didn't this make our leaders,
Macbeth and Banquo, afraid?
SOLDIER:
Yes; fearful
Like sparrows do eagles, or rabbits do lions.
However, honestly they fought
Like cannons with double ammunition;
They delivered twice as many blows at their enemies:
Unless they intended to bathe in warm, spilling blood,
Or re-live the horrors of some other battle,

I can't tell —

But I'm weak, my injuries are begging for attention.

DUNCAN:

Your words reflect your bravery, as do your wounds:

They both speak of honor.—Go, get him doctors.

Exit Soldier, with help. Enter Ross and Angus.

Who's approaching?

MALCOLM:

The respected Thane of Ross.

LENNOX:

How rushed he looks! He should only look this way

If he's about to give terrible news.

ROSS:

God save the King!

DUNCAN:

Where've you come from?

ROSS:

From Fife, noble king,

Where Norwegian flags laugh at our ground

And frighten our people.

The King of Norway himself, with a large army,

Assisted by the traitorous Thane of Cawdor, started a dreadful

battle;

Until Macbeth, prepared and fearless,

Faced him off, move for move

and, to end it,

The victory was ours.

DUNCAN:

Great joy!

ROSS:

Now Sweno, the King of Norway, begs for peace.

We refused to bury his soldiers

until he paid us ten thousand dollars.

This money will be used later for the common good.

DUNCAN:

The Thane of Cawdor will not trick us anymore.

Announce his death

and give his title to Macbeth.

ROSS:

I will ensure it's done.

DUNCAN:

What the Thane of Cawdor has lost, brave Macbeth has gained.

Exit.

SCENE III. A HEATH

FIRST WITCH:
Where were you, sister?

SECOND WITCH:
Killing pigs.

THIRD WITCH:
And where were you, sister?

FIRST WITCH:
There was a sailor's wife eating chestnuts,
Eating round after round. "Share some," I asked.
"Get away, witch!" the overfed woman yelled.
Her husband's gone to Aleppo, captain of the ship called "Tiger:"
I'll sail there by sneaking onto the boat,
And, like a tailless rat,
I'll do, I'll do, and I'll do.

SECOND WITCH:

I will give you a wind.
FIRST WITCH:
You're so kind.
THIRD WITCH:
And I'll give another.
FIRST WITCH:
I myself have all the rest,
Even the very directions they blow,
Every section of the ship's map they know.
I will dry him out:
Sleep won't come, day or night
On his eyelids;
He'll live a cursed life.
For seven weeks nine times over,
He'll grow weak, sickly, and fade:
His ship won't sink,
But it will be battered by storms.
See what I've got.
SECOND WITCH:
Let me see, let me see.
FIRST WITCH:
Here I have a ship captain's thumb,
Wrecked as he returned home...

A drum sounds.

THIRD WITCH:
A drum, a drum!
Macbeth is coming.
ALL:
The weird sisters, hand in hand,
Travelers of ocean and land,
Round and round we go:
Three times for yours, and three times for mine,
And three times again, to total nine.
Quiet!—the spell is complete.

Enter Macbeth and Banquo.

MACBETH:
Such a strange and eventful day, unlike any I've seen before.
BANQUO:
How far is it until we reach Forres Castle?
—Wow! Who are these ladies,
So wild they look not like ordinary beings?
Are you real?
Can we talk to you? You seem to understand us,
As each one of you puts a choppy finger to her thin lips.
You appear to be women, but your facial hair confuses me.
Are you really women?
MACBETH:
Speak. Who are you?
FIRST WITCH:
Greetings, Macbeth! Hail to you, Thane of Glamis!
SECOND WITCH:
Greetings, Macbeth! Hail to you, Thane of Cawdor!
THIRD WITCH:
Greetings, Macbeth! You're destined to be king!
BANQUO:
Why do you seem scared by something that sounds so magnificent?
Ladies, are you a figment of imagination, or real—
As you seem to be? You praise my noble friend
With high honors and predictions of future greatness,
and he seems interested in it. But you do not yet speak to me.
If you can see the future,
and determine what will come true and what will not,
Speak up now. I neither seek nor fear
Your approval or hate.
FIRST WITCH:
Hail!
SECOND WITCH:

Hail!

THIRD WITCH:

Hail!

FIRST WITCH:

You'll be less than Macbeth yet greater.

SECOND WITCH:

Not so happy, yet much happier.

THIRD WITCH:

You will father kings though you won't be one.

Hail, Macbeth and Banquo!

FIRST WITCH:

Banquo and Macbeth, greetings to you both!

MACBETH:

Wait... tell me more.

I know I'm the Thane of Glamis because of my father's death.

But how can I be the Thane of Cawdor?

The current Thane of Cawdor is alive.

And the thought of being king

Seems impossible,

Just like the thought of being Thane of Cawdor. Can you tell me

Where you got this information? Or why

You stop us on this path

With your mysterious predictions? I want answers.

Witches disappear.

BANQUO:

Just like the water has bubbles, so does the earth.

Where did they disappear to?

MACBETH:

They disappeared into thin air; and what seemed real

Disappeared like a breath in the wind.

I wish they'd stayed!

BANQUO:

Did we really just witness that?

Or did we eat something that made us hallucinate?

MACBETH:

Your children will be kings.

BANQUO:

But you will be king.

MACBETH:

And the Thane of Cawdor too-- is that not right?

BANQUO:

Exactly. Who's that coming our way?

Enter Ross and Angus.

ROSS:

The King is very happy, Macbeth,

To hear about your victory. And when he heard

About your bravery in the rebels' fight,

He couldn't decide who deserved more praise:

you or him. In the end, he was thankful.

In reviewing the rest of the day,

He found you

Fearless despite the overwhelming odds,

Facing death bravely.

Messages after messages came, each one

Praising your brave defense of the kingdom,

And singing your praises to him.

ANGUS:

We were sent

To bring you our king's gratitude;

And to bring you to him,

Not to pay you.

ROSS:

For a promise of a higher honor,

He instructed me to call you Thane of Cawdor:

Adding to your title, most deserving Thane,

Because it's yours now.

BANQUO:

What, can the witches speak truth?

MACBETH:
The Thane of Cawdor is alive: why do you give me this title?
ANGUS:
The Thane is alive, but
Facing serious punishment that he
rightfully deserves.
He is a traitor.
His crimes, admitted and proven,
Have defeated him.
MACBETH:
[Quietly thinking.] Thane of Glamis, and now Thane of Cawdor:
The best is yet to come. *[To Ross and Angus.]*
I appreciate your efforts.
[To Banquo.] Don't you have hopes your kids will be kings,
When those that made me Thane of Cawdor
Promised no less for your children?
BANQUO:
If you believe that,
It may spark hopes of you becoming a king,
Aside from being Thane of Cawdor. But be careful,
Dark forces often tell us truths
To trick us into hurting ourselves.
Let's chat for a moment.
MACBETH:
[Quietly.] Two truths have been shared,
Like a teaser to this grand story.
Thank you, sirs.
[Quietly again.] This supernatural prediction
Can't be bad, but it can't be good. If it's bad,
Why has it shown me a taste of success,
Beginning with a truth? I am now Thane of Cawdor.
If this is good, why do these images that give me goosebumps,
make my heart beat out of my chest?

The fears in my mind are less extreme
than these terrifying thoughts.
The idea of committing murder is just a fantasy,
yet the idea shakes up my state of being.
I've become so consumed by it that the world fades,
with only my strange reality taking hold.

BANQUO:
Just look at how Macbeth is distracted.

MACBETH:
[Quietly to himself.]
If fate wants me to be king,
then fate it will do it without me doing much.

BANQUO:
New responsibilities have landed on him,
similar to how our unfamiliar clothes don't quite fit
until we've worn them for a while.

MACBETH:
[Quietly to himself.] Whatever will be, will be.
Time and events will unfold,
regardless of how difficult the day might seem.

BANQUO:
Our respectable Macbeth,
we await your readiness.

MACBETH:
Please forgive me.
My brain is clouded with silly matters.
Kind sirs, your efforts are remembered,
and I'll reflect upon it every day.
Let's move towards the King
and ponder upon what's happened.
When there's more time available,
we'll share our thoughts with each other
after considering everything.

BANQUO:
Gladly, indeed.
MACBETH:
Until then, that's enough.
Let's go, my friends.

Exit

SCENE IV. FORRES. A ROOM IN THE PALACE

DUNCAN:

Has the sentence been carried out on the Thane of Cawdor?
Have those responsible not yet returned?

MALCOLM:

My king, they have not yet returned.
But I spoke with a witness who saw Cawdor's demise.
He told me that Cawdor admitted his betrayals with complete honesty, pleaded for your pardon, and expressed deep regret.
Nothing in his life became him more than the way he left it;
his death showed the same carelessness
with which one might discard an unimportant trinket.

DUNCAN:

It's impossible to read someone's thoughts just by looking at their face. I had put total trust in Cawdor.

Macbeth, Banquo, Ross and Angus enter.

My most worthy cousin!
I feel a heavy guilt that I haven't thanked you enough
for everything you've done.
You're so far ahead in your accomplishment
that even the quickest payback seems slow in reaching you.
I wish you had done less so that I could keep up with you.
All I can say is, you deserve more than anyone can repay.
MACBETH:
The services and loyalty that I offer to you,
pay themselves as I do them.
Your role, your Highness, is to accept our duties.
And our duties are to support your throne and country,
like loyal children and servants;
we are simply doing as expected,
acting always to secure your love and respect.
DUNCAN:
I extend a warm welcome to you here.
I have singled you out for special favor,
Macbeth, and I will make sure
To continue. Let me embrace you, Noble Banquo,
You've done no less than he and should be known for it.
BANQUO:
If I continue to do well, it is for you.
DUNCAN:
My joy is so great, it's almost overwhelming.
Family, closest advisors,
We will name Malcolm, our eldest son, as future king.
This honor will not make him special alone -
Others will also shine bright like stars with their deserving acts.
From here, we continue on to Inverness, and be bound to you
even more.
MACBETH:
The remaining task is my duty.

I'll announce myself and bring happiness in my wife with news of your arrival;

So, I humbly say goodbye.

DUNCAN:

My worthy Thane of Cawdor!

MACBETH:

[Aside.] The future king! That's an obstacle

That I must overcome or fail, for it blocks my path.

Stars, hide your light!

Do not expose my dark desires.

Let the hand move unseen, yet let it accomplish

What the eye fears to see, when it happens.

Exit.

DUNCAN:

True, worthy Banquo! He is full so brave;

Your praises nourish me. It is a feast to me. Let's follow him,

He's already making arrangements to welcome us:

He is an exceptional relative.

Flourish. Exit.

SCENE V. INVERNESS. A ROOM IN MACBETH'S CASTLE

13   *[Enter Lady Macbeth, who's reading a letter.]*

LADY MACBETH: *[reading]*

"They met me after we won the battle; and I've learned they possess more knowledge than any human being can. Just as my curiosity was about to lead me to question them further, they disappeared. While I was still trying to process what happened, I received messages from the King, who congratulated me as 'Thane of Cawdor'; a title given to me earlier by these three Weird Sisters. They hinted at a future where I would be hailed as the king! I felt it was necessary to inform you of these events (my dearest partner in greatness). I wanted you to share in the joy of what could be our shared greatness. Keep this close to your heart and remember it well."

Glamis you are, and Cawdor you will be,
Just as you've been promised.
Yet, I worry about your nature;

You seem too kind
To take the shortcuts to success.
You desire greatness,
Your ambition is not lacking, but you lack
The ruthlessness necessary for it.
You want great things,
And you want to achieve them in a noble manner;
You wouldn't cheat,
Yet you long to earn something you're not supposed to.
You'd like to have them, great Glamis.
Those feelings which urge, "This is what you must do,"
And that which you are afraid to do,
Will remain undone. Hurry over here,
So I can whisper my thoughts into your ear,
And strengthen you with the boldness of my words.
You are kept from your destiny,
Which fate and unnatural help seem
To promise you.

Enter a Messenger.

What news do you bring?
MESSENGER:
The King will be here tonight.
LADY MACBETH:
You must be crazy to say it.
Isn't your master with him? If so,
He should've informed us to become ready.
MESSENGER:
My apologies, but it is true. Our leader is coming.
A colleague of mine rushed back faster than him,
Who, out of breath and nearly dead, hardly had more
Words than were needed to deliver his message.
LADY MACBETH:
Take care of him.
He brings important news.

Exit Messenger.

The crow is hoarse
That tells of Duncan's doomed arrival here.
Come, you spirits
You feed on human thoughts, make me less like a woman here,
Fill me, from head to toe, overflowing
With terrible cruelty! Thicken my blood,
Prevent me from feeling guilt,
So that any natural empathy does not disturb
My violent plans, and stop me from acting.
Come to my breasts,
And turn my milk to poison, you murdering helpers,
Who wait unseen to commit evil! Come, black night,
And shroud yourself in the darkest smoke of hell
So that my sharp knife cannot see the wound it makes,
And heaven can't see the crime through the darkness
And cry out, "Stop, stop!"

Enter Macbeth.

Honored Glamis, noble Cawdor!
Greater than both, by the future praise!
Your letters have moved me beyond
This ignorant present, and I feel now

MACBETH:
My love,
Duncan is arriving tonight.

LADY MACBETH:
And when does he plan to leave?

MACBETH:
He plans to leave tomorrow.

LADY MACBETH:
Oh, he should never see that day!
Your face, my lord, is like an open book that gives away everything.
To fool everyone,

Act normal and
make sure to have a welcoming look in your eyes,
in your hand, and your words: appear innocent as a flower,
But be sly like a snake hiding under it.
The visitor arriving must be taken care of;
and tonight's important event you should leave up to me to
manage;
Tonight shall control our nights and future days
Giving us complete power and control.
MACBETH:
We shall discuss this further.
LADY MACBETH:
Just stay positive;
It will sour your mood to be afraid.
I'll do everything else.

Exit.

SCENE VI. THE SAME. BEFORE THE CASTLE

 [Hautboys. Macbeth's servants attending.]

Enter Duncan, Malcolm, Donalbain, Banquo, Lennox, Macduff, Ross,
Angus and Attendants.

DUNCAN:
This castle has a welcoming feel. The air
Gently and sweetly comes to to us.
BANQUO:
This guest of summer,
The martlet bird, seems to think the same,
By making its nest in these very walls because the air here
Is pleasing: there's no feature in particular that makes it better
for nesting,
But this bird has chosen to make its bed and breed.
Where these birds flock and live, I've noticed
The air is always crisp and delicate.

Enter Lady Macbeth.

DUNCAN:

Look, our honored hostess!—

The love that others display can sometimes bring us trouble,

Yet, we're grateful for it. So, here's a lesson for you

In how to thank God for the efforts you've made,

And express gratitude for any inconvenience.

LADY MACBETH:

All our work,

Reviewed twice, and then done once more,

Would still seem like nothing compared

To the great honor

Your Majesty brings to our home.

We remain your gracious hosts.

DUNCAN:

Where's the Thane of Cawdor?

We followed him closely,

but he's a good horseman!

And his deep affection for you has helped him

To reach home before us. Our gracious and noble hostess,

We are your guests tonight.

LADY MACBETH:

Your servants always

They always keep in mind what is needed and stay

Ready for a check at your command,

Always intending to give what belongs to you.

DUNCAN:

Please, give me your hand;

Take me to our host: we hold him in great respect,

And we'll continue showing him our good graces.

With your permission, hostess.

Exit.

SCENE VII. THE SAME. A LOBBY IN THE CASTLE

18 [*MUSICIANS AND TORCHBEARERS LEAD THE WAY. ENTER, AND PASS BY, A SERVER AND VARIOUS SERVANTS WITH DISHES FOR THE FEAST. THEN, MACBETH ENTERS.*]

MACBETH:
If the deed is to be done, better it get done quickly. If the murder
Could succeed,
this act alone
Might be everything—here,
But here, in this unstable moment of time,
We risk our future. And in decisions like these
We have to use our better judgement; when we teach
Violent actions, they can come back
To trouble the one who acted. This fair justice
Passes poison in the cup
Back to the one who prepared it. He is doubly trusted:
Firstly, because I am his cousin and his subject,
Both of which make me against the act; and secondly, as his host,

Who should protect him from his killer, not be the one holding
the knife. And then, this Duncan,

So gentle in his rule, so clear in his duties, that his good qualities
Will defend him, like angels, loudly against
The awful damnation of his murder;
And pity, like a innocent newborn,
Bravely against the winds, or heaven's cherubim, flying
Upon the swift messengers of the air,
Will spread the terrible deed to all,
Until tears will drench the wind.—I have no motivation
except a strong ambition, which overleaps itself
And trips—

Enter Lady Macbeth.

What's the latest?

LADY MACBETH:

He's nearly finished his meal. Why did you leave the room?

MACBETH:

Did he ask for me?

LADY MACBETH:

Don't you know that he has?

MACBETH:

I'm not going to go through with this plan:
He has shown me respect lately, and I've earned
The respect of all different kinds of people,
Which I would like to hold onto, not throw away so soon.

LADY MACBETH:

What happened to your earlier commitment?
Did it disappear since then?
And does it get smaller and smaller now, to appear so weak and
scared
At what you so willingly agreed to do? From this moment
I consider your love this way. Are you afraid
To act with the same courage you have in desire? Don't you
want that

Which you hold as the prize of life? Or will
You live as a coward in your own eyes?
Letting "I dare not" control "I would,"
Like the cat from the old saying?
MACBETH:
Please, stay calm!
I dare do what is necessary for a man;
Those who dare do more don't exist.
LADY MACBETH:
What stopped you, then,
From keeping your promise to me?
When you dared to do it, then you were a man;
And to be more than what you were, you would
Be so much more the man. Neither the right time nor place
Were with us then, and yet you would make them both:
They've presented themselves, and that's what makes you hesi-
tant now.
I have nursed a child, and know
How deeply it makes me want to care for the child that feeds
from me:
I would, while it was smiling at me,
Have ripped my nipple from its gumless mouth.
And ended its existence, if I made the same promise as you
Have done to me.
MACBETH:
What if we fail?
LADY MACBETH:
We fail?
Strengthen your bravery,
And we won't fail. When Duncan is asleep
His two guards
I will get so drunk with wine and a holiday punch mix
That their memories,
Will be in a daze, and their ability to think clearly

Will be done for:
Then what can't you and I do to
The undefended Duncan? They shall carry the blame
For our actions.
MACBETH:
My dear, you're fit only to give birth to boys;
Your fearless spirit should create
Only men. So it will be thought,
When we have marked them with blood,
and used their own blades,
That they have done it?
LADY MACBETH:
Who would dare think otherwise,
Since we shall pretend to be heartbroken
at the announcement of the king's death?
MACBETH:
I am committed, and ready.
Let's go, and cover our intentions with nice looks:
A deceiving face must hide what a deceitful heart knows.

Exit.

ACT II

SCENE 1. INVERNESS. COURT WITHIN THE CASTLE

[BANQUO AND FLEANCE ARRIVE, THE PATH LIT BY THEIR TORCH.]

BANQUO:

What's the time, Fleance?

FLEANCE:

The moon has set.

BANQUO:

Indeed.

FLEANCE:

I believe, it's already past midnight, sir.

BANQUO:

Hold on, take my sword.

The heavens are saving their resources,

all their lights are off.

I feel so tired, as if there's a heavy burden on me,

but I do not wish to sleep.

May the higher powers keep away

the evil thoughts that come to one in sleep!

Macbeth enters with a servant.

BANQUO:
Who goes there?
MACBETH:
A friend.
BANQUO:
Oh, haven't you gone to bed yet?
The King's already resting.
He's been enjoying the night and
has generously rewarded your staff.
He's also sent a diamond with a note for your wife,
addressing her as his gracious hostess and
expressing his endless satisfaction.
MACBETH:
Caught off guard by the King's arrival,
we did the best we could.
BANQUO:
Nonetheless, all seems well.
I had dreams of the three witches last night.
They have told some truth to you.
MACBETH:
I haven't given much thought to them or their predictions.
But, if we could find a suitable time to discuss this further,
I would appreciate it.
BANQUO:
Whenever you find the time.
MACBETH:
And if you agree with me when the time comes,
it will bring you honour.
BANQUO:
As long as I don't lose any of my honour in trying to increase it,
I will try to be loyal.
BANQUO:
But, if I'm free and clear in my loyalty,

I'll be happy to talk and take your advice.
MACBETH:
Sleep well for now!
BANQUO:
Thanks, and you too.

Exit Banquo and Fleance. Enter Servant.

MACBETH:
Tell your lady, when my drink is ready,
To ring the bell. Go to bed.

Exit Servant.

Is that a dagger I see before me,
the handle pointing towards my hand?
Come, let me hold it. I can't grasp you, but I still see you.
Are you a real weapon or just a dagger of the imagination,
a trick played by my stressful mind?
I can still see you, as clear as anything I might touch or hold.
You're pointing me towards the path I was planning to take,
and you're the tool I intended to use.
My eyes are tricking all my other senses,
or but usually they're the only ones worth trusting.
I still see you, and I see droplets of blood on your blade that
weren't there before. This is all just my imagination.
Now half of the world seems to be asleep,
filled with nightmares.
The witches are making their dark offerings,
and murder, woken by the watchful wolf,
is sneaking forward with silent steps, like a ghost.
You, firm earth, don't make a sound.
Don't let anyone know I'm here,
don't take away the frightful atmosphere of this moment.
While I talk, he still lives.
But my words aren't as powerful as my actions.

A bell rings.

I'm going, and it will be done. The ring of the bell is my invitation.

Don't hear it, Duncan, for its sound is like a toll
Calling you to your destiny, whether that be heaven or hell.

Exit.

SCENE 11. THE SAME

 [Enter Lady Macbeth.]

LADY MACBETH:

The same thing that made them drunk has motivated me:

The drink that knocked them out has sparked my courage.
Listen! Quiet!

It was the owl's shriek, like a night watchman,

Shouting the harshest goodnight. He's doing it now.

The doors are open; the servants

Are snoring, neglecting their duties: I drugged their drinks,

And now death and life are in a battle over them,

Arguing whether they should live or die.

MACBETH:

[From the inside.] Who goes there? Hey!

LADY MACBETH:

Oh no, I'm scared they've woken up,

And it's not finished. Starting but not completing

The act is messing with us. Listen!—I left out their daggers;

He couldn't have missed them. If Duncan hadn't looked
Like my father in his sleep, I would have done it myself. My husband?

Enter Macbeth.

MACBETH:

I've done it.—Didn't you hear a noise?

LADY MACBETH:

I heard the owl screech and the crickets chirping.

Did you say something?

MACBETH:

When?

LADY MACBETH:

Just now.

MACBETH:

As I was coming down?

LADY MACBETH:

Yes.

MACBETH:

Listen!—Who's in that second room?

LADY MACBETH:

Donalbain.

MACBETH:

This is a distressing sight.

Looking at his hands.

LADY MACBETH:

Silly to call it distressing.

MACBETH:

One of them laughed in his sleep,

And another cried, "A murder!"

They startled each other awake: I stood and listened to them.

But then they said their prayers and fell back asleep.

LADY MACBETH:

Those two are staying in the same room.

MACBETH:

One of them said,
"God bless us!" and the other responded, "Amen,"
As though they'd seen me with these murderer's hands.
Hearing their fear, I wasn't able to say "Amen,"
After they wished, "God bless us."
LADY MACBETH:
You're thinking about it too much.
MACBETH:
But why wasn't I able to say "Amen"?
I was in need of a blessing, and "Amen"
Just wouldn't come out of my mouth.
LADY MACBETH:
Don't dwell on your actions in that way,
It'll drive us crazy.
MACBETH:
It seemed I heard a voice say, "No more sleep!
Macbeth has murdered sleep"—the innocent sleep;
Sleep, which untangles the twisted knots of worry,
The ending of each day's stress, the cure for hard labor,
Comforter of troubled minds, nature's healing touch,
Main provider in life's comfort.
LADY MACBETH:
What are you talking about?
MACBETH:
Still the voice said, "No more sleep!" to the whole house:
"Macbeth has murdered sleep, so now nobody
Will sleep anymore. Macbeth himself will never sleep again!"
LADY MACBETH:
Who was crying out? Dear lord,
You're letting your imagination run wild. Go get some water
And wash the evidence of this deed from your hand.—
Why did you bring these daggers from there?
They should stay there: go put them back, and stain
The sleeping servants with blood.

MACBETH:
I won't go back there:
I'm scared to even think about what I've done;
I dare not look at it again.
LADY MACBETH:
What a weakling!
Give me the daggers. The sleeping and the dead
Are mere images. It's only children who
One of them said,
"God bless us!" and the other responded, "Amen,"
As though they'd seen me with these murderer's hands.
Hearing their fear, I wasn't able to say "Amen,"
After they wished, "God bless us."
LADY MACBETH:
You're thinking about it too much.
MACBETH:
But why wasn't I able to say "Amen"?
I was in need of a blessing, and "Amen"
Just wouldn't come out of my mouth.
LADY MACBETH:
Don't dwell on your actions in that way,
It'll drive us crazy.
MACBETH:
It seemed I heard a voice say, "No more sleep!
Macbeth has murdered sleep"—the innocent sleep;
Sleep, which untangles the twisted knots of worry,
The ending of each day's stress, the cure for hard labor,
Comforter of troubled minds, nature's healing touch,
Main provider in life's comfort.
LADY MACBETH:
What are you talking about?
MACBETH:
Still the voice said, "No more sleep!" to the whole house:
"Macbeth has murdered sleep, so now nobody

Will sleep anymore. Macbeth himself will never sleep again!"
LADY MACBETH:
Who was crying out? Dear lord,
You're letting your imagination run wild. Go get some water
And wash the evidence of this deed from your hand.—
Why did you bring these daggers from there?
They should stay there: go put them back, and stain
The sleeping servants with blood.
MACBETH:
I won't go back there:
I'm scared to even think about what I've done;
I dare not look at it again.
LADY MACBETH:
What a weakling!
Give me the daggers. The sleeping and the dead
Are mere images. It's only children who

SCENE III. THE SAME

 [The Porter walks in as knocking continues off-stage.]

PORTER:

The knocking is near constant, as though a man were the gate-keeper of Hell himself, constantly turning the key. *[Knocking.]* Knock, knock, knock. Who's there, in the name of the beast himself? Ah, a farmer who took his own life, expecting riches: timely arrival; make sure you have enough handkerchiefs; you're going to sweat for this. *[Knocking.]* Knock, knock! Who's there, in another demon's name? Ah, it's a deceiver, who could swear deceitfully on all sides, betrayed his own people enough for holy retribution, yet couldn't deceive his way to heaven: Come forth, deceiver. *[Knocking.]* Knock, knock, knock! Who's there now? Ah, it's an English tailor who's come here for thievery from a Frenchman's wardrobe: come forth, tailor; roasting awaits you here. *[Knocking.]*Knock, knock. It's never peaceful here! Who are you? —However, this place is too chilly for the underworld. I won't play the devil's gatekeeper any longer: I had planned to welcome people from every profession, the ones following the pretty path to the eternal bonfire. *[Knocking.]* In a moment, in a moment! Do keep in mind the gatekeeper, won't you?

Opens the gate. Macduff and Lennox walk in.

MACDUFF:

Did you retire late, friend, that you rise so late?

PORTER:

In truth, sir, we were celebrating till the crow of the second rooster; and drinking, sir, tends to provoke three major things.

MACDUFF:

What three things does consuming strong drink bring?

PORTER:

Well, a man drinking too much can get quite a red nose, make him sleepy, and have him spending a lot of time in the bathroom. As for lust, it both stirs it up and causes problems - it can make a man want to, but can also be bad. So, it's like alcohol and lust are at odds: they push him forward, but then knock him back down; they encourage him, only to disappoint him; they make him ready to go, but then undermine his strength. Basically, it tricks him with sleep and, after making a fool of him, leaves him there.

MACDUFF:

I think you drank too much last night, huh?

PORTER:

Yes, sir. But I paid it back for its deception; and (I think) I still managed to stand my ground.

MACDUFF:

Is your master awake?

Enter Macbeth.

You've been knocking a while, so he's probably up.

LENNOX:

Good morning, sir!

MACBETH:

Morning to you both!

MACDUFF:

Is the King up, honorable thane?

MACBETH:

Not yet.

MACDUFF:

He told me to wake him early.

I've almost missed the time.

MACBETH:

I'll take you to him.

MACDUFF:

I know this is a happy task for you;

But it still is a task.

MACBETH:

We love him, so it's no worry.

Here's his room.

MACDUFF:

I'll go ahead and wake him up.

It's my duty, after all.

Exit Macduff.

LENNOX:

Is the King leaving today?

MACBETH:

Yes, that's what he arranged.

LENNOX:

This past night was wild: at our place, the chimneys toppled over, and, I've heard it said, there were cries of death in the wind, weird shrieks

And people predicting

Of terrible fires and messes,

Recently introduced to these troubled times.

Some are saying that there was an earthquake.

MACBETH:

It was a rough night.

LENNOX:

I can't recall a night similar.

Enter Macduff.

MACDUFF.

Oh, what a horrific scene!

Neither words nor the heart can understand or describe.

MACBETH and **LENNOX**:

What's going on?

MACDUFF:

Chaos has truly shown its nasty face!

A murder most awful has destroyed

God's sanctuary, and taken life.

MACBETH:

What are you saying? The life?

LENNOX:

Do you mean the King?

MACDUFF:

Come closer to the room, and prepare your sight

For a new horror. Don't ask me to explain further.

See, and then speak for yourselves.

Macbeth and Lennox exit.

Awake, awake! —

Sound the alarm bell. — Murder and betrayal!

Banquo and Donalbain, Malcolm! Wake up!

Look at death face to face! Get up, get up, and see

The image of ultimate doom. Malcolm! Banquo!

Rise to bear witness to this horror!

The alarm bell rings.
Enter Lady Macbeth.

LADY MACBETH:

What is all this?

The whole house is woken by this bell.

Tell me, tell me!

MACDUFF:

Oh dear lady,

It's not right for your ears to hear what I have to say:

Hearing it spoken again, in a woman's ear,

Would kill her instantly.

Enter Banquo.

Oh Banquo, Banquo!
Our king's been killed!
LADY MACBETH:
Oh no!
What, in our house?
BANQUO:
Too cruel.—
Macduff, please, say it's not true,
And tell us it's a lie.

Enter Macbeth, Lennox, and Ross.

MACBETH:
If I had died just one hour before this happened,
I would have lived a happy life; but now,
Nothing in life is important anymore.
Everything is meaningless:
The best part of life is past, and it only leaves
A bitter aftertaste.

Enter Malcolm and Donalbain.

DONALBAIN:
What's going on?
MACBETH:
You're in danger and don't even know it:
Someone has targeted your family; the source of your bloodline
has been cut off.
MACDUFF:
Your royal father's been murdered.
MALCOLM:
Oh, by whom?
LENNOX:
It seemed to be his own servants:
Their hands and faces were all covered with blood;
Their daggers too, which we found

on their pillows, still bloody.

MACBETH:

Oh, I do regret that my anger

Led me to kill the servants.

MACDUFF:

Why did you do that?

MACBETH:

Who can be controlled and outraged,

Loyal and indifferent, all at once? No one.

I had a deep love for Duncan

And I didn't stop to think. Here was Duncan,

His white skin covered with his golden blood;

And his deep wounds...

And there, the murderers,

With their daggers soaked from the bloody act!

Who could hold back,

If they had love in their heart,

And in that heart the bravery to admit it?

LADY MACBETH:

Oh my goodness, I'm sick.

MACDUFF:

Please, attend to the lady.

MALCOLM:

Why are we silent?

DONALBAIN:

What should be said here?

Anything could happen.

Let's go even though our tears haven't been shed yet.

MALCOLM:

It's as though our sadness

Can't move us to act.

BANQUO:

Attend to the lady.

Lady Macbeth is carried out.

49

Let's gather
And discuss this gruesome deed
To better understand it. Fears and doubts shake us:
I stand under the protection of God; and from there
I fight against the betrayal we need to discover.
MACDUFF:
And so do I.
ALL:
So all of us.
MACBETH:
Let's quickly get determined
And assemble in the hall altogether.
ALL:
Agreed.

Malcolm and Donalbain remain.

MALCOLM:
What's our plan? Let's not join them:
If we stay, we could be next. I'll go to England.
DONALBAIN:
I'll go to Ireland. Our respective fortunes
Will keep us safer. Here among us,
There's bitterness hidden beneath friendly faces.
MALCOLM:
This is just the beginning and our safest plan
Is to dodge the aim. Quickly, to our horses;
And let's not hang around in saying goodbye,
Let's get out of here. There's no compassion left.

Exit.

SCENE IV. THE SAME. WITHOUT THE CASTLE

 [Enter Ross and an Old Man.]

OLD MAN:

I remember things well from the past seventy years,

In all that time I have seen

Terrifying hours and weird events, but never anything like this terrible night

Which makes previous events seem insignificant.

ROSS:

Oh, wise father,

You see the sky, troubled by man's actions,

Threatens his path: according to the clock it is daytime,

And yet it's like nighttime.

Is it that the darkness is stronger than the light,

or should we be ashamed of the day?

When it allows the earth to be in darkness,

When the warm sunlight should be there?

OLD MAN:

This is unnatural,
Just like the terrible act that was committed. Last Tuesday,
A falcon, sitting in her high position,
Was attacked and killed by a common owl.
ROSS:
And then, a strange and certain thing: Duncan's beautiful and fast horses,
Usually so tame, suddenly went wild, broke out of their stables,
As if they wanted to go to war with human beings.
OLD MAN:
I heard they turned on each other.
ROSS:
They did; the sight of it was shocking.
But here comes the noble Macduff.

Enter Macduff.

What's happening in the world, Macduff?
MACDUFF:
Can't you tell?
ROSS:
Do we know who committed this horrible act yet?
MACDUFF:
It was the men Macbeth killed.
ROSS:
Oh, what a terrible day!
How could they even justify such a thing?
MACDUFF:
They must have been bribed.
Malcolm and Donalbain, the King's two sons,
The children have run away, which only makes them look guilty.
ROSS:
It's against nature:
Ambition which is wasteful, can consume
Your whole life! —Then it's likely
That Macbeth will become king.

MACDUFF:

He is already named, and he's gone to Scone

To be officially crowned.

ROSS:

Where is Duncan's body?

MACDUFF:

Taken to Colmekill,

The resting place of his ancestors.

ROSS:

Are you heading to Scone?

MACDUFF:

No, cousin, I'll go home to Fife.

ROSS:

Alright, I'll be going there.

MACDUFF:

Alright, may you see things being done properly there. Goodbye!

May our old clothing be more comfortable than our new ones!

ROSS:

Goodbye.

OLD MAN:

May God's blessing go with you; and with those

Who would turn bad into good, and enemies into friends!

They all exit.

ACT III

SCENE 1. FORRES. A ROOM IN THE PALACE

 [Banquo enters.]

BANQUO:

You have it all now, king, Cawdor, Glamis,

just like the strange ladies predicted.

I'm worried you did some terrible things to get to this point.

And yet, they said that your children would not be kings.

That I, myself, would be the origin and father of many kings to come.

If their predictions turned out to be true for you, Macbeth,

why shouldn't I hope they'll come true for me as well?

But I should keep quiet for now.

Fanfare. Macbeth enters as King, along with Queen Lady Macbeth;
Lennox, Ross, Lords, and attendants.

MACBETH:

Our main guest has arrived.

LADY MACBETH:

If we had forgotten him,

it would have left a hole in our grand feast.
MACBETH:
Tonight, we're holding a royal dinner Banquo,
and I want you to be there.
BANQUO:
If it's your command, then I will obey.
My responsibility to you is unbreakable.
MACBETH:
Are you going for a ride this afternoon?
BANQUO:
Yes, my lord.
MACBETH:
We would have asked for your wise advice
in today's meeting, but we can wait till tomorrow.
How far are you riding?
BANQUO:
As far as I can between now and dinner.
If my horse isn't up to it,
I'll need to borrow the darkness for a couple of hours.
MACBETH:
Don't miss our dinner.
BANQUO:
My lord, I won't.
MACBETH:
Our traitorous cousins are hiding out,
In England and in Ireland, without telling
Their crimes and spreading lies.
But we'll talk tomorrow,
Ride on your horse without delay.
Goodbye until your return at night.
Fleance is going with you, right?
BANQUO:
Yes, my king: we are due to leave now.
MACBETH:

I hope your horses are fast and reliable;
And so, I wish you a good journey.
Farewell.

Banquo exits.

Until seven at night,

every person is free to do as he pleases.

We will keep ourselves alone until supper time.

That will make later on, much better.

Until then, may God be with you.

Exit Lady Macbeth, the Lords, and others.

You there, please come here, are those men waiting to meet us?
SERVANT:

Yes, my king,

they are outside the palace gate.
MACBETH:

Call them here.

Servant exits.

Being the king is worth nothing if it's not safe.

I fear Banquo deeply;

His nature is so noble that it makes me afraid.

He's definitely brave,

and has the wisdom

To act carefully.

There's no one else I'm afraid of: with him around

I feel second best, just like they say

Mark Antony felt with Caesar.

Banquo condemned the sisters

When they first crowned me king,

And asked them to speak to him;

Then they proclaimed him

As the father of future kings.

They placed a fruitless crown upon me,

And put an empty scepter in my hand,

To be stolen away by someone not of my blood,

59

No son of mine following. If it is so,
I've poisoned my brain for the sake of Banquo's children;
For them I committed the terrible murder of noble Duncan;
Planted troubles inside myself
Only for their sake;
To make them kings, make Banquo's offspring kings!
Rather than that, come, let destiny control
And defend me till the end!—Who's there?—

Enter Servant with two Murderers.

Go to the door, and wait there till we summon you.

Exit Servant.

Was it not just yesterday that we spoke?

FIRST MURDERER:

Yes, it was, your Highness.

MACBETH:

Well then, now.
Have you thought about our conversation?
It was Banquo, in the past, who placed you
In such a terrible position, which you though had been
My innocent self? I clarified this to you
In our most recent meeting, discussing with you
How you were misled and manipulated to make
You understand and say, "Banquo did this."

FIRST MURDERER:

You made it clear to us.

MACBETH:

I did and this is why
We're meeting for the second time. Do you find
Your patience so strong
That you can let this slide? Are you so moral,
To pray for this respectable man and his children,
When his actions have led you to your downfall,
While making you poor forever?

FIRST MURDERER:

We are men, my lord.

38 **MACBETH:**
Yes, technically you are "men;"
Just as there are "dogs" –
Hounds, greyhounds, mongrels, spaniels, curs,
Odd breeds and wolves.
The different kinds separate the quick, the slow, the clever.
They are different
Even though they all share the same general label: "dog."
The same can be said of men.
Now, if you see yourselves somewhere within this list,
Not at the very bottom of humans, then speak;
I have a task which means getting rid of an enemy,
A task that will bring you into my good graces,
Since our well-being is impacted by his life,
Which in his death, would be restored.
SECOND MURDERER:
I am one, my lord,
So angered by the world's harsh treatment
That I don't care what happens next.
FIRST MURDERER:
And I'm another,
So frustrated with life's trials and struggles,
That I'd gamble all just to improve my life or end it.
MACBETH:
Both of you know Banquo was your enemy.
BOTH MURDERERS:
True, my lord.
MACBETH:
Indeed, he's my enemy too.
His very existence threatens my well-being.
I can eliminate him outright,

And make my desire a reality, but I should not do it,
Because of friends that he and I share,
Whose trust I cannot betray.
I am seeking your help,
Hiding this task from public view
For many important reasons.
SECOND MURDERER:
We will, my lord,
Carry out your orders.
FIRST MURDERER:
Even if it costs us our lives—
MACBETH:
Your determination shows. Within this hour,
I will guide you where you need to be,
Inform you of the perfect opportunity,
It must be done tonight
I need assurance
That everything is clear. Alongside him
(To leave no mistakes or flaws in the task)
Banquo's son, Fleance, who is with him,
Must also die.
Take some time apart to prepare.
I will come to you soon.
BOTH MURDERERS:
We are ready, my lord.
MACBETH:
I'll call you soon: wait indoors.

Exit Murderers.

The deal is done. Banquo, if your soul
Is to find heaven, it must go tonight.

Exit.

SCENE 11. THE SAME. ANOTHER ROOM IN THE PALACE

 [Enter Lady Macbeth and a Servant.]

LADY MACBETH:
Has Banquo left?

SERVANT:
Yes, madam, but he'll be back tonight.

LADY MACBETH:
Please tell the King that I would like to speak with him
When he has a moment to spare.

SERVANT:
Madam, I will.

Exit.

LADY MACBETH:
When you achieve your goal but don't feel happy,
It's better to be destroyed,
Than to live in fear after causing destruction.

Enter Macbeth.

How are you, my lord? Why do you choose to be alone,
Bothered by negative thoughts?
These worries should have died along with what caused them.
What's done is done.
MACBETH:
We have wounded the snake, not killed it.
In time, it will heal, and we are still worried about its bite.
But we would rather see the world fall apart,
And experience the world's wrath,
Rather than live with fear and nightmares every night.
It's better to be at peace with the dead,
Those we ended to find our peace,
Than to always have concerns, causing a lack of sound sleep.
Duncan rests in peace in his grave.
Life's troubles have come to end for him.
Whatever harm could have been done has been done.
Nothing can touch him anymore.
LADY MACBETH:
Come on,
Calm down, my lord, soften yourself,
Be cheerful and friendly with your guests tonight.
MACBETH:
I will try, my love; and I hope you will, too.
Remember to give Banquo lots of attention,
With both your eyes and your words.
Yet it's dangerous for us
To have to pretend this way,
To hide our true feelings behind fake smiles.
LADY MACBETH:
You need to let this go.
MACBETH:
Oh, my mind is filled with troubling thoughts, dear wife!
Banquo and his son Fleance are still alive.
LADY MACBETH:

But their time on earth isn't forever.
MACBETH:
That's a relief; they can be taken care of.
Then cheer up. Before the night is over,
A horrible act will be completed.
LADY MACBETH:
What needs to be done?
MACBETH:
It's better you don't know, my dear,
Until it's completed. Come on, cloak of night,
Hide the gentle light of day.
And with your invisible hand,
Destroy the fear!
The light is fading; and the crow
Flies off to the dark woods.
The good things of day start to fade and grow tired,
While the creatures of the night awaken to hunt.
You're surprised at my words: but be patient;
So, please, come with me.

Exit.

SCENE III. THE SAME. A PARK OR LAWN, WITH A GATE LEADING TO THE PALACE

42 *[Enter Three Murderers.]*

FIRST MURDERER:
Who asked you to join us?

THIRD MURDERER:
Macbeth did.

SECOND MURDERER:
We can trust him. He's given us our orders and what we need to do.

FIRST MURDERER:
Then stand with us.

Our target is getting closer.

THIRD MURDERER:
Listen! I can hear horses.

BANQUO: *(Call from offstage.)*
A light, someone give us a light!

SECOND MURDERER:
It's him.

The others who were expected have already gathered.

FIRST MURDERER:

His horses are going around.

THIRD MURDERER:

It's about a mile, but most people,

including him, walk from here to the palace gate.

Banquo and Fleance enter carrying a torch.

SECOND MURDERER:

A light! We need a light!

THIRD MURDERER:

It's him.

FIRST MURDERER:

Let's get ready.

BANQUO:

I think it's going to rain tonight.

FIRST MURDERER:

Let it come down.

Attacks Banquo.

BANQUO:

Oh no! Treachery! Run, Fleance, run!

You can seek revenge—oh no!

Banquo dies. Fleance escapes.

THIRD MURDERER:

Who blew out the light?

FIRST MURDERER:

Was that not the plan?

THIRD MURDERER:

Only one is down:

the son has escaped.

SECOND MURDERER:

We have lost the more significant part of our plan.

FIRST MURDERER:

Let's leave and report back.

Exit.

43

SCENE IV. THE SAME. A ROOM OF STATE IN THE PALACE

44   *[A FEAST IS READY. ENTER MACBETH, LADY MACBETH, ROSS, LENNOX, LORDS AND THEIR HELPERS.]*

MACBETH:

Please take your seats.

I want to personally welcome each and every one of you.

LORDS:

Thank you, your Majesty.

MACBETH:

I will join the gathering,

And act the gracious host.

Our hostess maintains her modesty; but, when the time is right,

We will all appreciate her hard work.

LADY MACBETH:

Please express my gratitude for me, sir, to all our friends;

For I really feel they are welcome.

Enter the First Murderer at the door.

MACBETH:

See, they greet you with their gratitude.
We're all equals here: I'll sit right in the middle.
Enjoy and be merry;
soon we'll toast around the table.

Approaching murderers.

I see blood on your face.
MURDERER:
It's Banquo's blood.
MACBETH:
It's better you're stained with it than Banquo is.
Is he taken care of?
MURDERER:
My lord, Banquo is dead. I did it.
MACBETH:
You're the best of the bunch.
Yet the one who kills Fleance will also be appreciated.
If you manage it, you'll have no equal.
MURDERER:
My noble sir,
Fleance escaped.
MACBETH:
Here comes my fear again:
I would have been fine otherwise;
Solid like marble, sturdy like a rock,
Open and free as the surrounding air:
But now I'm trapped, limited, chained,
To fears. But is Banquo really gone?
MURDERER:
Yes, my lord. Banquo lies in a ditch,
With twenty deep cuts on his head;
The minimum required by nature.
MACBETH:
Thank you for that update.

Fleance will grow and
Has the potential to become dangerous in time,
For now, he's harmless.—Leave now; we will
Talk more on this matter tomorrow.

Exit Murderer.

LADY MACBETH:
My respected lord,
You're not entertaining your guests:
a dinner is considered poor
If it isn't appreciated while it's being prepared,
A warm reception is half the feast.

The Ghost of Banquo appears, and takes Macbeth's seat.

MACBETH:
An unexpected reminder!—
Now, may good digestion accompany a healthy appetite,
And well-being follow them both!

LENNOX:
Would you please take your seat, your Highness?

MACBETH:
We could have fully been celebrating our country's honor,
If only our esteemed Banquo was here;
I wish he was here.

ROSS:
My lord,
His absence reflects negatively on his loyalty. Might we please
Have the pleasure of your company, Highness?

MACBETH:
But the table's already full.

LENNOX:
There's a space saved right here, sir.

MACBETH:
Where?

LENNOX:
Right here, my good lord.

Is something bothering you, Highness?

MACBETH:

Who among you has pulled this prank?

LORDS:

What are you referring to, my lord?

MACBETH:

Don't you dare

Flaunt those bloody signs at me.

ROSS:

Gentlemen, stand; our leader is not well.

LADY MACBETH:

Sit, respected friends. My husband sometimes gets like this,

And it's been this way since his youth: Please, stay seated;

He will recover quickly...

If you pay him too much attention,

you will only upset him more and extend his fit.

Eat, and don't focus on him. ---Are you a man?

MACBETH:

Yes, and a brave one.

I can look at things that would scare the devil himself.

LADY MACBETH:

Honestly, you're overreacting!

This is just like when you thought

you saw the floating dagger that led you to Duncan.

You're imagining things again.

These sudden scares would make a good story

for a woman to tell around a fire,

but they are ridiculous coming from you.

Why are you acting so scared?

You're just looking at a stool anyhow.

MACBETH:

Please, look there! See that?

What do you have to say now?

Why should I care?

If those we've buried are destined to return.

Ghost disappears.

LADY MACBETH:

Are you completely losing your mind?

MACBETH:

If I'm standing here, then I saw him.

LADY MACBETH:

Shame on you!

MACBETH:

There has been bloodshed in the past,

before laws were established to protect the weak.

Since then horrific murders have occurred.

There once was a time when, if the brain was out,

the man would die and that would be it.

But now, they come back to life,

committing more deadly murders,

and pushing us from our seats.

This is stranger than any murder.

LADY MACBETH:

My darling husband,

our noble friends are missing you.

MACBETH:

I forgot.

Please don't look at me like that, my valuable friends.

47 I HAVE A STRANGE SICKNESS, but it's no surprise

to those who know me.

Now, let's toast to love and good health for all.

I'll join you.

I drink to the joy of everyone at this table,

and to our much-missed friend Banquo. I wish he were here.

The Ghost appears again.

Here's to everyone, including him!

LORDS:

To all!

MACBETH:

Go away! Get out of here! Hide yourself on earth!

Your bones are empty, your blood is cold.

You don't see anything with those eyes you stare with!

LADY MACBETH:

Don't worry about this, kind lords.

This is just his habit. It's nothing else.

MACBETH:

Sure, whatever a man dares, I dare:

If I tremble then, call me a scared child.

Hence, horrible ghost, unreal mockery, go away!

Ghost disappears.

Now that it's gone,

I feel like myself again.—Please, everyone, stay seated.

LADY MACBETH:

You've upset the party.

MACBETH:

Can things like this really happen,

And take over us as quickly as a summer's cloud?

It's strange to me

To think you can see such things,

And remain calm as mine go pale with fear.

48 **ROSS**:

What have you seen, my lord?

LADY MACBETH:

Please, don't speak; his condition worsens;

Asking questions only angers him. Say goodnight—

Don't wait for the perfect moment to leave,

Just go, now.

LENNOX:
Goodnight; and may better health
Be with His Majesty!
LADY MACBETH:
A heartfelt goodnight to everyone!

All the nobles and attendants leave.

MACBETH:
They say blood will have blood.
Even rocks are known to move, and trees to talk,
revealing the most secretive man of violence.
—What time is it?
LADY MACBETH:
Almost at odds with dawn, it's hard to tell.
MACBETH:
What do you say,
that Macduff is absent on such a big day?
LADY MACBETH:
Did you send for him, sir?
MACBETH:
I've heard some things.
There's not one of them in whose house
I don't clothe and feed...
I'll go tomorrow to the Weird Sisters:
They will reveal more to me;
For now, I am bent on knowing,
By any means necessary,
The worst case scenario. For my own safety,
All reasons will be put aside: I am so steeped in blood
That turning around is just as tiresome as moving forward.
I have strange things in my mind, turning into actions,
Which must be carried out before they can be thoroughly
thought out.
LADY MACBETH:

You are lacking the best of all resources, sleep.
MACBETH:
Let's go to bed.
Our journey to rule is merely in early stages.

They exit.

SCENE V. THE HEATH

49 *[THUNDER. THE THREE WITCHES MEET HECATE.]*

FIRST WITCH:
Hecate, why the angry look?
HECATE:
Do I not have a reason, you old hags?
You dare to deal with Macbeth,
Meddling in riddles and matters of death;
And I, who is the master of your magical arts,
The hidden maker of all troubles,
Was never asked to play my role,
Or reveal the power of our craft?
He only cares for his own benefit, not for you.
Now you must correct your wrongs: be off,
And meet me at the pit of Acheron
In the morning: he will come there
To learn about his fate.
Prepare your potions and your spells,

Your magic, and all other things.
I'll travel through the air; this night I'll spend
On a grim and fatal task.
Important work must be completed by noon.
There, on the edge of the moon
A misty drop is hanging;
I'll collect it before it falls to the ground:
And that, refined by magical tricks,
Will bring such ghosts,
Which, through the strength of their illusion,
Will lead him to his downfall.
He will defy fate and act foolishly.

Music and song within, "Come away, come away."

Hear that! I am called; my little spirit, you see,
Sits in a foggy cloud and waits for me.
Exit.

FIRST WITCH:
Let's hurry, she'll return soon.

Exit.

SCENE VI. FORRES. A ROOM IN THE PALACE

51   *[Enter Lennox and another Lord.]*

LENNOX:
Things have been oddly carried out. The noble Duncan
Was pitied by Macbeth: interestingly, he was dead:
And the brave Banquo was out too late;
Whom, you might say, if it pleases you, Fleance killed,
Because Fleance ran away. People shouldn't be out too late.
Who cannot consider, how terrible
It was for Malcolm and for Donalbain
To murder their noble father? Damned deed!
How it upset Macbeth! Didn't he immediately,
In a rage, seek revenge on the two
Who were drunk and sleepy slaves?
Wasn't that nobly done? Yes, and wisely too;
For it would have infuriated anyone,
To hear the men deny it. So, I say,
He has handled all matters well: and I believe,

That if he had Duncan's sons under his control
(Though, heaven forbid, he won't)
They would understand
What it means to kill a father;
So should Fleance.
But, silence!
Because of some words exchanged,
And because he failed
To attend the tyrant's feast, I'm told,
Macduff has a target on him. Sir, do you know
Where he's hiding?
LORD:
The son of Duncan,
Whom this tyrant has robbed of his rightful title,
Lives at the English court and is welcomed
By King Edward with such respect
That no bad fortune can touch his reputation.
That's where Macduff is.
Has left to seek the king's support.
To get help from the armies
So, with their aid (and with God's blessing,
To sanction this deed), we might once again
Enjoy meals at our tables, peaceful sleep at night;
Our feasts and banquets free of blood,
Loyally serve, and receive rightful honours,
All things we desire now. This news
Has so angered the King that he
Prepares for war.
LENNOX:
Did he send for Macduff?
LORD:
He did: and with a firm "No, sir,"
The messenger turned his back,
And grumbled, as if to say, "You'll regret

The moment you burdened me with this answer."
LENNOX:
And that very well could
Advise him to be careful.
Hopefully a messenger will
Get to England's to warn him
Before he arrives,
so Scotland can be helped.
LORD:
I'll send my prayers along with him.

Exit.

ACT IV

SCENE 1. A DARK CAVE. IN THE MIDDLE, A CAULDRON BOILING

 [*A boom of thunder. The three Witches enter.*]

FIRST WITCH:
The striped cat has meowed three times.
SECOND WITCH:
Three times, and a hedgehog's whine.
THIRD WITCH:
A monster cries:—It's time, it's time.
FIRST WITCH:
Around the cauldron we go;
In it, throw the toxic guts.—
Toad, resting under cool stone
For 31 days and nights,
Has gathered a lot of venom while sleeping,
Boil it first in the charmed pot!
ALL:
Double, double, toil and trouble;
Fire, burn; and cauldron, bubble.

SECOND WITCH:
The meat from a murky water snake,
In the cauldron, let it bake;
Newt's eye, and frog's toe,
Bat's wool, and dog's tongue,
Adder's fork, and a blind worm's sting,
Lizard's leg, and owl's wing,
For a spell of immense trouble,
Let it boil and bubble like a wicked broth.
ALL:
Double, double, toil and trouble;
Fire, burn; and cauldron, bubble.
THIRD WITCH:
Dragon's scale, wolf's tooth,
A witch's mummy, the giant jaw and stomach
Of the plundering sea shark,
Hemlock root dug up in the darkness,
Liver of a lying person,
Goat gall, and yew tree bark
Stripped during the moon's eclipse,
Nose of a Turk, and lips of a Tartar,
Finger of an unceremoniously born baby
Make the soup thick and lumpy:
Add to it a tiger's stomach,
For our cauldron's ingredients.
ALL:
Double, double, toil and trouble;
Fire, burn; and cauldron, bubble.
SECOND WITCH:
Cool it with baboon's blood.
Then the spell is strong and set.

54   *Hecate arrives.*

HECATE:
Well done! You've worked hard,

And everyone will share the rewards.

Now, around the cauldron sing,

Casting magic on all that you put in.

Music and a song: "Black Spirits." Hecate leaves.

SECOND WITCH:

A sense of doom,

Something evil is arriving...

Unlock the doors,

For whoever is knocking!

Macbeth comes in.

MACBETH:

What's going on, you secretive witches!

What are you doing?

ALL:

Something that can't be named.

MACBETH:

I'm asking you, by the magic you claim,

(However you began to understand it) answer me:

Even if you untangle the turbulence of the wind, and let it battle

Against the churches; even if massive waves

Engulf and confuse the sea travelers;

Even if crops are knocked down, and trees uprooted;

Even if castles crash onto their guards' heads;

Even if grand buildings and pyramids lean

Until they crumble; even if all of nature's creations

Collapses into chaos,

Do answer me, no matter what I ask of you.

FIRST WITCH:

Speak.

SECOND WITCH:

Ask.

THIRD WITCH:

We'll answer your questions.

FIRST WITCH:

Tell me, whether you prefer to hear from us directly,
Or from our leaders?
MACBETH:
Call them, I wish to meet them.
FIRST WITCH:
Pour in the blood of a female pig, that has consumed
Her nine piglets; fat that has dripped
From the hangman's gallows, throw it
Into the fire.
ALL:
Come, high or low;
Display your power and work swiftly!

    Thunder. A vision of an armed Head appears.

55   **MACBETH:**
Tell me, mysterious force--
FIRST WITCH:
It knows what you are thinking:
Listen to its message, but don't speak.
FIRST APPARITION:
Macbeth! Macbeth! Macbeth! Be warned about Macduff;
Beware the Thane of Fife.—Leave me alone.—That's enough.

    Vanishes.

MACBETH:
Whatever you are, thank you for your wise advice;
You've hit on my exact worries.—But one more thing.
FIRST WITCH:
It will not be controlled. Here's another,
Stronger than the first.

    Thunder. A vision of a bloody Child appears.

SECOND APPARITION:
Macbeth! Macbeth! Macbeth!
MACBETH:
If I had three ears, I'd listen to you.
SECOND APPARITION:

Be strong, bold, and firm. Dismiss
The fear of any man, for none born of a woman
Shall harm Macbeth.

Vanishes.

MACBETH:
If that's the case, Macduff: why should I fear you?
But I'll secure everything. You won't live;
So I can prove my fear wrong,
And sleep despite the thunder.
Thunder. A vision of a Child crowned, with a tree in his hand, appears.
What is this being,
That rises as if it's a king's offspring,
And wears a crown on its infant forehead?
ALL:
Listen, but don't respond to it.
THIRD APPARITION:
Be as brave as a lion, proud, and don't worry
Who is angry, who is irritated, or where the traitors are:
Macbeth won't be defeated, until
Great Birnam forest marches towards lofty Dunsinane hill
To battle him.

Vanishes

.

MACBETH:
That is impossible:
Who can move a forest, command a tree...
Could one uproot a tree from the earth? Impossible, so good
for me!
I can live out his natural lifespan, pay his dues
To time and human tradition. Yet, I yearn
To know one thing: tell me, if you possess the power
To have so much, will Banquo's children ever
Rule this kingdom?
ALL:

Don't seek to know more.
MACBETH:
I won't be ignored: reject me this,
And may you forever be cursed! I need to know.
Why is that cauldron sinking? And what is that noise?

Musical instruments.

FIRST WITCH:
Show!
SECOND WITCH:
Show!
THIRD WITCH:
Show!
ALL:
Show him, and let him
Come and go like a shadow!

A parade of eight kings appears, the last holding up a mirror. Banquo is seen afterwards.

MACBETH:
You are too much like the ghost of Banquo. Begone!
Your crown burns my vision:—and your hair,
The other golden crown, too much like the first.
A third is just as similar.—Wicked witches!
Why are you showing me this?—A fourth!—Eyes, be alert!
Will this lineage continue until the end of time?
Another one!—A seventh!—I refuse to see more:—
But then an eighth appears, carrying a mirror
That pictures many more; and some I notice
Are bearing double orbs and triple scepters.
Horrifying imagery!—Now I see it is true;
Blood-stained Banquo is smiling at me,
And points to them as his own.—What! Is this reality?
FIRST WITCH:
Yes, sir, all of this is fact, but why
are you so shocked?

Come on, sisters, let's uplift his spirits,
And reveal to him our greatest spells.
I'll call forth a sound from the air,
While you perform your lively round;
So that this worthy king may kindly acknowledge,
Our acts served to greet him well.

Music. The Witches dance, and disappear.

MACBETH:
Where have they gone?—May this moment
Forever be cursed in our memories!—
Come inside, whoever is outside!

Enter Lennox.

LENNOX:
What's do you need, sir?
MACBETH:
Did you see the Weird Sisters?
LENNOX:
No, sir, I did not.
MACBETH:
Didn't they pass by you?
LENNOX:
No, certainly not, sir.
MACBETH:
May the air they travel on be cursed;
And may doom find all those who trust them
—I heard
The sound of horses' hooves: who was it that passed?
LENNOX:
Sir, it was two or three messengers who bring you news
That Macduff has fled to England.
MACBETH:
Fled to England!
LENNOX:
Yes, indeed, sir.

MACBETH:
Time, you're faster than my fearful deeds:
I need to take action. From this moment on
The very first thoughts in my mind will become
The first actions of my hand.
I'll ambush Macduff's castle;
Claim Fife; give to the sharp edge of the sword
His wife, his children, and all the unlucky ones
That follow him. No need for foolish boasting;
I'll complete this act while my motivation is still hot:
But no more visions!—Where are these men?
Come, bring me where they are.

Exit.

SCENE 11. FIFE. A ROOM IN MACDUFF'S CASTLE

   [ENTER LADY MACDUFF, HER SON, AND ROSS.]

LADY MACDUFF:

Why did he do it?

Why did he leave the country?

ROSS:

You must wait and understand, madam.

LADY MACDUFF:

He did nothing of the sort.

His decision to leave was thoughtless.

ROSS:

You're not aware

If it was his wisdom or his fear that led him.

LADY MACDUFF:

Intelligence! To abandon his wife, his children,

His home, and his titles, in a place

Which he himself is running from? He does not love us:

He lacks the basic instinct; even the tiny wren,

The smallest of all birds, will fight,
To protect her young ones against the owl in her nest.
It's all out of fear, and there's no love,
Just as there's no intelligence, where flight
Goes against logic.
ROSS:
My dear cousin,
I urge you to control yourself: but as for your husband,
He is noble, wise, and knows best
What suits the situation. I dare not elaborate:
But it's a harsh time when we suspect ourselves of treachery,
And don't understand who we are; when we believe rumours
Because of what we fear, yet we don't know what our fear is,
But instead drift on a stormy sea
Tossed by every wave and current — I shall take my leave of you:
I won't be away long, I'll be back soon.
My sweet cousin,
I wish you well!
LADY MACDUFF:
Yes, he has a father, but he's as good as fatherless.
ROSS:
I'll be a fool if I stay any longer,
I'd be embarrassed, and you'd be uneasy:
I must leave now.

Exit

LADY MACDUFF:
Dear boy, your father's dead.
What will happen now? How will you survive?
SON:
Like birds do, mother.
LADY MACDUFF.
What, would you eat worms and bugs?
SON:

Whatever I find, that's what I mean; and that's what birds do too.

LADY MACDUFF:

Poor thing! You wouldn't be scared of traps?

SON:

Why would I be, mother? These aren't meant for poor birds.

My father is not dead, no matter what you say.

LADY MACDUFF:

Yes, he is dead: who will be your father now?

SON:

If he is, then who will be your husband?

LADY MACDUFF:

Well, I could find myself multiple husbands if I went to the market.

SON:

So, you'd buy them, only to sell them again?

LADY MACDUFF:

You're speaking as smart as you can be.

Yet, in truth, you're just about witty enough for your age.

SON:

Was my father a traitor, mother?

LADY MACDUFF:

Yes, unfortunately, he was.

SON:

What is a traitor?

LADY MACDUFF:

A traitor is someone who breaks promises and lies.

SON:

So, does everyone who does this become a traitor?

LADY MACDUFF:

Yes, anyone who does this is a traitor and they're punished by hanging.

SON:

And everyone who lies or breaks promises should be hanged?

LADY MACDUFF:
Every single one of them.
SON:
But who should do the hanging?
LADY MACDUFF:
The honest men, of course.
SON:
Then the liars are being foolish:
there are enough of them to defeat
the honest men and hang them instead.
LADY MACDUFF:
May God help you, poor child! But how will you manage without
a father?
SON:
If he were truly dead, you'd cry for him: but if you didn't, it's a
sure sign that I'd have a new father soon.
LADY MACDUFF:
Oh, you little chatterbox, the things you say!

Enter a Messenger.

MESSENGER:
Wish you well, kind woman! It's true you don't know me,
Yet in your high status, I hold respect for you.
I fear that danger is near you:
If you will listen to a simple man's warning,
Do not stay here; escape, with your little ones.
To scare you like this is quite harsh;
Doing worse would be unthinkable,
It's too close to harming you in person.
May the heavens keep you safe!
I cannot remain any longer.

He leaves.

LADY MACDUFF:
Where should I escape to?
I have done nothing wrong. But now I remember

I am in this world, where doing wrong

Is often rewarded; doing right is sometimes

Seen as foolish risk: so why then, oh no,

Do I defend myself in this feminine way,

To say I have committed no wrong? Who are these men?

Enter Murderers.

FIRST MURDERER:

Where is your husband?

LADY MACDUFF:

I hope he's in a place so sacred

That you couldn't possibly find him.

FIRST MURDERER:

He's a traitor.

SON:

You're lying, you awful villain!

FIRST MURDERER:

What, you brat!

He stabs him.

Just a young product of treachery!

SON:

He's killed me, mother:

Run, I beg you!

He dies. Lady Macduff runs off, crying out "Murder!" and being chased by the Murderers.

SCENE III. ENGLAND. BEFORE THE KING'S PALACE

61   *[ENTER MALCOLM AND MACDUFF.]*

MALCOLM:
Let's look for a quiet place and there
Empty our hearts by crying.

MACDUFF:
Instead,
Let's hold tightly to our swords, and, like brave men,
Defend our threatened homeland.
Scotland's hurt, and shouts out
In words of sorrow.

MALCOLM:
This tyrant, whose name is painful to say,
Was once thought good: you were fond of him;
He hasn't wronged you yet. I am young; but maybe
You could earn his favor through me; and wisdom
In sacrificing a harmless, innocent lamb
To calm an angry god.

MACDUFF:

I am not a traitor.

MALCOLM:

But Macbeth is.

A good and noble nature may falter

Under great stress. But I must apologize.

My thinking can't really change who you are.

Angels are bright still, even the brightest one fell:

Even if all bad things seemed good,

Goodness must still look like itself.

MACDUFF:

I have lost all hope.

MALCOLM:

Perhaps even where I had my doubts.

Why did you leave your wife and child,

Those dear reasons, those strong bonds of love, behind?

Without saying goodbye? Please,

Don't let my suspicions offend you,

They're for my own safety. You could be right,

No matter what I think.

MACDUFF:

Oh, poor country, bleed!

Tyranny, make your claim,

For goodness can't stand against you! Take on the wrongs,

The title is settled.—Take care, lord,

I would not be the traitor you suspect

For all the power within the tyrant's reach

And all the riches of the East.

MALCOLM:

Don't be upset:

I'm not speaking out of total fear of you.

In my opinion, our country is oppressed;

It cries, it bleeds, and every day adds
Another scar to its injuries. I also believe
That people would support my rightful claim;
And here, from generous England, I have received
Offers of great support: but even so,
When I overthrow the tyrant,
Or claim my throne, my poor country
Will suffer more than ever before,
More pain, and in more different ways,
By the person who will take over.

MACDUFF:

And who would that be?

MALCOLM:

I'm speaking of myself; I know that
I have so many problems of my own,
That, when exposed, evil Macbeth
Will seem as innocent as snow; and the poor country
Would prefer him, as gentle as a lamb,
Compared with my limitless harms.

MACDUFF:

Not even the worst monsters
Of hell can produce a devil more cursed
In wickedness to overtake Macbeth.

MALCOLM:

I see him as awful,
Excessive, greedy, dishonest, deceitful,
Quick to act, evil, full of every sin.
But I have a flaw that has no name: there's no end, none,
In my indulgences: your wives, your daughters,
Your matrons, and your girls, wouldn't satisfy
The store of my desires.
Therefore, Macbeth is better
Than I as such a one to rule.

MACDUFF:

Uncontrolled indulgence
In one's desires has caused
The downfall of joyful rulers,
And led to the ruin of many kings. But don't fear yet
To embrace what's rightfully yours: you could
Enjoy your pleasures,
And still seem reserved—the times can be deceiving.
We have enough willing women; you can't possibly
Have that great of an appetite.
MALCOLM:
And along with this, there grows
In my most ill-organized passions, such
A greed that, if I were king,
I'd strip the nobles of their estates;
Crave his jewels, and want someone else's house:
And my greed would only fuel my hunger;
Leading me to stir up false quarrels against the good and faithful,
Destroying them for wealth.
MACDUFF:
This greed
Is more deep-seated; grows with a more harmful touch
Than lust; and it has caused
The downfall of our fallen kings: yet do not fear;
Scotland has resources to satisfy your desires,
It all belongs naturally to you. All these can be taken,
Balanced with other instances of grace.
MALCOLM:
But I have none: the qualities best for a king,
Such as justice, truth, moderation, and reliability,
Generosity, determination, mercy, humility,
Dedication, patience, bravery, courage,
I have none of them, rather, I overflow
With every type of wrongdoing,
Practicing them in numerous ways. If I had the power,

64

I'd pour the sweet milk of harmony into chaos,
Disturbing the peace, creating
Disorder everywhere.
MACDUFF:
O Scotland, Scotland!
MALCOLM:
If someone such as me is fit to lead, tell me:
I can only be what I've said.
MACDUFF:
Fit to lead?
No, not even fit to live. - O my poor nation,
Suffering under a tyrant,
When will you see your brighter days again?
Given that the true heir to your throne
Is a victim to so many problems,
And slanders his family name? Your royal father
Was a good king, the queen who gave birth to you,
More often on her knees than on her feet,
Died a little each day she lived. Farewell!
The bad deeds you've cast upon yourself
Have driven me from Scotland. - O my heart,
My hope stops here!
MALCOLM:
Macduff, your passion,
Born of honesty, has removed the dark doubts from my soul.
Aligned my thoughts with your truth and nobility. Evil Macbeth
Has tried several strategies to draw me under his rule.
Modesty has pulled me back
From being too quick to believe: but let God above
Decide between us! For even now,
I offer myself to your guidance, and
Withdraw my own self-criticism; here I give up
The flaws and faults I've imposed on myself.
I remain a stranger to my true self. To this day,

I've never been disloyal;
I've hardly ever wanted what was already mine,
Never did I break my promise; would not even betray
The devil to his companion; and find joy
No less in truth than in life: I lied to you
About myself. What I truly am,
Is at your and our poor country's disposal:
In fact, even before you arrived here,
Old Siward, with ten thousand soldiers,
Ready to fight, was already marching towards us.
Now we'll get together, and the possibility of success
To save our beloved country. Why are you silent?
MACDUFF:
It's hard to understand such welcome
and unwelcome news at the same time.

A Doctor enters.

MALCOLM:
Well, we'll discuss more later. — Is the king coming out, I
beg you?
DOCTOR:
Yes, sir. A group of souls
Are awaiting his healing: their sickness challenges
The best efforts of medicine; but with his touch,
They immediately improve.
MALCOLM:
I thank you, doctor.

Doctor leaves.

MACDUFF:
What's the sickness he's referring to?
MALCOLM:
It's known as the evil:
A most miraculous work by this good king;
Which often, since my stay in England,
I have witnessed him do. How he calls upon heaven,

He himself best knows. Yet, the sick people,
Inflamed and suffering from ulcers, a pitiful sight,
Beyond any surgeon's help, he cures;
Hanging a golden necklace around their necks,
Blessed by holy prayers: and it's said,
That he passes on this healing blessing
To the future royalty. With this strange power,
He has a heavenly gift of prophecy;
And numerous blessings surround his throne,
Showcasing his tremendous grace.

Enter Ross.

MACDUFF:
Look, who's this?
MALCOLM:
My fellow countryman; but I can't quite see.
MACDUFF:
Welcome, my ever polite cousin.
MALCOLM:
Ah, I recognize him now. Dear God, please remove
All obstacles such as these!
ROSS:
Indeed, sir.
MACDUFF:
Is Scotland still holding up?
ROSS:
Well, our poor country,
Almost seems afraid of its own condition! It's no longer
Our motherland, but our burial ground, where only those,
Who are ignorant, ever appear to be happy;
Where cries of pain echo in the air,
Go unheard; because sadness is
A common thing. The tolling bell
Barely concerns for whom it tolls; and good people
Pass away before it is natural.

MACDUFF:

Oh, your words

Cut deep but they carry truth!

MALCOLM:

What's the latest misfortune?

ROSS:

Recent news stirs up the rumor mill;

Each passing minute brings a new one.

MACDUFF:

How is my wife?

ROSS:

She is well.

MACDUFF:

And my children?

ROSS:

They are well too.

MACDUFF:

The ruler hasn't disturbed them?

ROSS:

No; they were living in peace when I last saw them.

MACDUFF:

Speak freely: What's the situation?

ROSS:

When I arrived to deliver the news,

Which has weighed heavily on me, there was a rumor

About many respectable people pushing back against Macbeth;

It seemed possible to me,

As I have seen the ruler's power in action.

Now's the time for help. Your presence in Scotland

Will inspire soldiers, even encourage our women to fight,

To free themselves from their terrible difficulties.

MALCOLM:

We're on our way there to bring them help.

Generous England has

Given us the great General Siward and ten thousand troops;
There isn't a more experienced or skilled soldier
In all of Christian Europe.
ROSS:
I wish I could respond with equal good news! But I carry news
That should be yelled
Where no ear should hear them.
MACDUFF:
What do these words concern?
Are they about the general conflict? Or a specific grief
tied to just one person?
ROSS:
No honest heart is exempt from some sorrow, though the major
part of this sorrow belongs to you alone.
If it's about me,
Don't withhold it, tell me at once.
ROSS:
Please don't hate me for what I'm about to say,
For it's the heaviest news
You've ever heard.
MACDUFF:
Hmm, I think I know what it is.
ROSS:
Your home has been ambushed; your wife and children
Have been brutally killed. To describe how it happened
Would only deepen your pain.
MALCOLM:
Heaven help us!—
Don't hide your sorrow. Give your grief a voice. The grief that
remains silent
Hurts the overfilled heart, and commands it to break.
MACDUFF
Were my children also killed?
ROSS:

Everyone—your wife, children, servants—
Anyone who could be found there.
MACDUFF:
And I wasn't with them!
Was my wife killed too?
ROSS:
Yes, I've said so.
MALCOLM:
Note your heart;
Let's turn our desire for revenge into a force for healing.
To heal this deadly sadness.
MACDUFF:
He doesn't have any children. All of my beautiful ones?
Did you say all of them? Oh, heartless monster! All?
All of my lovely children and their mother
Gone in one terrible moment?
MALCOLM:
Handle this like a man.
MACDUFF:
I will; but I must also feel it as a man.
I can't help but remember them,
Those that were most precious to me. Did God see this,
And not step in to help? It's my fault, sinful Macduff
They were all killed because of me!
Not for their own wrong doings but due to mine,
This terrible fate fell upon their innocent souls.
May heaven give them peace now!
MALCOLM:
Turn this sadness into anger. Let sadness
Turn into anger; don't let your heart be dulled, ignite it with rage.
MACDUFF:
Oh, I could cry like a woman,
And boast with my words! But, kind heavens,
Cut short any delay; face to face,

Bring this evil man from Scotland and myself together;
Put him within reach of my sword; if he escapes,
May heaven forgive him too!
MALCOLM:
You talk like a true man.
Let's go to the King. Our strength is ready;
The only thing we lack is the permission to proceed. Macbeth
Is ready for a fall, and the powers from above
Are prepared. Take whatever comfort you can;
The night is long that never finds the day.

They exit.

ACT V

SCENE 1. DUNSINANE. A ROOM IN THE CASTLE

⁶⁹ *[A DOCTOR ENTERS, ALONG WITH A WOMAN GENTLEWOMAN.]*

DOCTOR:

We've both spent two nights watching, and yet I don't see any truth to your reports. When did she last sleepwalk?

GENTLEWOMAN:

Ever since the King left for the battlefield, I've observed her get out of bed, throw on a nightgown, unlock her cabinet, take out some paper, fold it, write on it, read it, seal it, and then get back into bed. And amazingly, she does all this while completely asleep.

DOCTOR:

How strange that she can sleep yet also show signs of being awake. In her sleepy state, aside from walking and these other actions, have you ever heard her say anything?

GENTLEWOMAN:

What she has said, I don't want to repeat.

DOCTOR:

You can tell me.

GENTLEWOMAN:

No, I can't tell you nor anyone else, as there's no one else to verify my word.

Lady Macbeth enters carrying a candle.

Look, here she is, sleepwalking just as I've described. Notice her; stay close.

DOCTOR:

How did she get the candle?

GENTLEWOMAN:

It was already by her side. She's asked to have constant access to light.

DOCTOR:

I see her eyes are open.

GENTLEWOMAN:

Yes, but she can't see anything. She is asleep.

DOCTOR:

What's she doing now? Look, she's rubbing her hands.

GENTLEWOMAN:

70   This is a consistent behavior for her, to pretend to wash her hands like this. I've seen her do it for fifteen minutes at a time before.

LADY MACBETH:

There's still a stain here.

DOCTOR:

Listen, she's talking. I'll note down everything she says, so that I remember it better.

LADY MACBETH:

Out, cursed spot! Out, I command! One, two. It's time. Hell is a dark place! Shame, my lord, shame! A soldier and afraid? What do we have to fear when no one knows our deeds and no one can question us? Who would have thought the old man had so much blood in him?

DOCTOR:

Did you hear that?

LADY MACBETH:

The thane of Fife had a wife. Where is she now? What, will my hands never be clean? Stop that, my lord, stop that. You ruin everything by reacting this way.

DOCTOR:

Enough, enough. You've heard what you shouldn't have.

GENTLEWOMAN:

She has said what she shouldn't have, I'm certain of that. Only heaven knows what she's witnessed.

LADY MACBETH:

I can still smell the blood. Not even all the perfumes of Arabia can mask this smell on my hand. Oh, oh, oh!

DOCTOR:

Hear that sigh! Her heart is heavy with guilt.

GENTLEWOMAN:

I wouldn't want such a pained heart for all the world.

DOCTOR:

Well, well, well...

GENTLEWOMAN:

Let's hope for the best, sir.

GENTLEWOMAN:

This condition is beyond my expertise. However, I have seen sleepwalkers who were pure at heart and went on to die peacefully in their beds.

LADY MACBETH:

Clean your hands, get your nightgown on; don't look so white. I'll tell you again, Banquo's in the ground; he can't rise from his grave.

DOCTOR:

Is that so?

LADY MACBETH:

To bed, to bed. There's knocking at the door. Come, give me your hand. What's been done can't be reversed. To bed, to bed, to bed.

Exit.

DOCTOR:

Is she going to bed now?
GENTLEWOMAN:
Straight away.
DOCTOR:
Bad rumors are spreading. Unnatural acts
Create unnatural problems. Minds filled with guilt
Will reveal their secrets to their deaf pillows.
She needs a spiritual guide more than a doctor.—
God, forgive us all! Take care of her;
Take away everything that bothers her,
And always watch over her. So, good night:
She's filled my mind with confusion, and surprised my eyes.
I have thoughts, but don't dare to speak.
GENTLEWOMAN:
Good night, kind doctor.

Exit.

SCENE 11. THE COUNTRY NEAR DUNSINANE

 [Enter thanes, Menteith, Caithness, Angus, Lennox, and their soldiers, with their gear ready for battle.]

MENTEITH:

The English forces are coming, led by Malcolm,

His uncle General Siward, and the honorable Macduff.

They want revenge; their just reasons

Could make even a religious man fight.

ANGUS:

We will meet them near Birnam wood.

That's where they're headed.

CAITHNESS:

Does anyone know if Donalbain is with his brother?

LENNOX:

He most definitely isn't. I have a list

Of all the men: there's Siward's son

And many young soldiers, who are just now

Experiencing their first war.

MENTEITH:
What's the tyrant doing?
CAITHNESS:
He's heavily protecting great Dunsinane.
Some say he's crazy; others, who don't dislike him as much,
Call it fearless bravery: but one thing's for sure,
He can't control his chaotic situation.
ANGUS:
Now he feels
The weight of his secret murders;
The people he betrayed coming back to him;
Those under his rule obey only because they have to,
Not out of loyalty: now he feels his title
Is unstable and ill-fit, like small thief
who tries to wear a large coat.
MENTEITH:
Then I'm sure he really
Is nervous and jumpy.
Everything within him knows
He shouldn't be there.
CAITHNESS:
Alright, let's keep moving,
To show our loyalty where it's due:
And cure our troubled nation;
And alongside him, we contribute to our country's cleansing.
Each one of us.
LENNOX:
Or as much as required
To help the rightful ruler and get rid of the problems.
Let us advance towards Birnam.

They exit, marching.

SCENE III. DUNSINANE. A ROOM IN THE CASTLE

 [Enter Macbeth, Doctor, and Attendants.]

MACBETH:
No more updates, let them all go:
Until the Birnam forest relocates to Dunsinane,
I will not be fearful. What about young Malcolm?
Wasn't he born from a woman? The spirits who know
The outcomes of everything have told me this:
"Do not fear, Macbeth, no man born from a woman
Will ever have control over you." So flee, deceitful lords,
And blend with the English:
The mind I listen to, and the heart I carry
Will never shake with doubt nor fear.

Enter servant.

Curse you, you pale-faced fool!
Where did you get that foolish look?
SERVANT:
There are ten thousand ssss—

MACBETH:
Geese, you rascal?
SERVANT:
No, soldiers, sir.
MACBETH:
Go pinch your face and exaggerate your fear,
You cowardly boy. What soldiers, you fool?
You're scared to the bone! Your scared, pale face...
What soldiers, you coward?
SERVANT:
The English army, as you asked sir.
MACBETH:
Get out of my sight.

Exit Servant.

Seyton! Inside, I'm feeling off,
When I notice—Seyton, I command!—This challenge
Will either energize me always or dishearten me now.
I've lived long enough: my lifestyle
Falls like a withered, yellow leaf;
And what normally comes with getting older,
Like respect, love, obedience, a battalion of friends,
I can't have; instead, in their place,
Silent curses, superficial respect, and false praises--
75   Which the desperate heart rejects yet can't refuse.
Seyton!—

Enter Seyton.

SEYTON:
What can I do for you, sir?
MACBETH:
Is there any more news?
SEYTON:
Everything that was reported is true.
MACBETH:
I'll fight until my bones are stripped of flesh.

Bring me my armor.
SEYTON:
It's too early, sir.
MACBETH:
I insist on putting it on.
Dispatch more horses, let them investigate the surrounding countryside;
Hang those who speak of fear. Give me my armor.—
How is your patient, doctor?
DOCTOR:
She's not really sick, my lord.
She has haunting thoughts
That keep her from resting.
MACBETH:
Heal her of that.
Can't you help to a troubled mind,
Erase the sadness of her memory,
Eliminate the brain's troubles,
with a soothing medicine?
DOCTOR:
Regarding this illness, the patient
Must heal herself.
MACBETH:
Medicine is useless.
Come, help me with my armor, hand me my staff:
Seyton, take action.—Doctor, my lords abandon me.—
Quickly, sir.—If you could, doctor, treat
The illness of my land, identify the disease,
And cleanse it to a healthy and original state,
I would praise you so loud that even the echo
Would echo back. —Take it off, I demand.—
What medicine,
Would drive these English away? Have you heard of any?
DOCTOR:

Yes, my good lord. Your royal preparations
Tells us of some news.
MACBETH:
I will carry it with me—
I will not fear death or harm,
Until Birnam forest moves to Dunsinane.

Everyone leaves except the Doctor.

DOCTOR:
If I could get away from Dunsinane,
Not even money could bring me back here.

He leaves.

SCENE IV. DUNSINANE. WITHIN THE CASTLE

 [THE REBEL SCOTTISH FORCES HAVE JOINED MALCOLM'S ARMY AT BIRNAM WOOD.]

MALCOLM:

Cousins, I hope we can soon be safe.

MENTEITH:

We hope so too.

SIWARD:

What forest is this before us?

MENTEITH:

Birnam Forest.

MALCOLM:

Let every soldier cut down a tree branch and hold it in front of him.

We can shadow our numbers and Macbeth won't know

How many soldiers we have.

SOLDIERS:

It shall be done.

SIWARD:

We've heard the confident tyrant

Stays in Dunsinane, and will receive us there.

MALCOLM:

He hopes to be successful,

But I have heard many people serve him,

But they do so without any real loyalty.

MACDUFF:

Let's not judge before we get there.

SIWARD:

The time is now.

We shall find out soon what's to come of this.

We know for certain that we must fight.

So, let's advance to war.

Exit.

SCENE V. DUNSINANE. WITHIN THE CASTLE.

78 *[ENTER MACBETH, SEYTON, AND SOLDIERS, FOLLOWING THE RHYTHM OF DRUMS AND FLAGS.]*

MACBETH:

Hang our war flags on the castle walls;

The shout is, "They approach!" Our castle's strength

Will laugh at any attack: let them stay here

Until starvation and disease consume them.

If their army wasn't reinforced by traitors,

We could've courageously faced them, eye to eye,

And driven them back whence they came.

Women scream in the background.

What is that noise?

SEYTON:

It's the scream of women, my lord.

Exit.

MACBETH:

I've nearly forgotten what fear feels like.

There used to be a time when my senses would've shuddered
To hear a scream like that; and my hair
Would stand on end at terrifying tales
However, I have engaged in so many terrors, and
Horrific scenes in my murderous thoughts,
That I can't even flinch now.

Enter Seyton.

What caused that scream?
SEYTON:
The Queen, my lord, is dead.
MACBETH:
She should have did later.
There would have been an appropriate time for such news.
Tomorrow, and tomorrow, and tomorrow,
Closes in each day,
Up to the last moment of known time;
And all our days gone by have made fools
Navigate the path to their own end. Enough, enough, brief life!
Life's like a fleeting shadow; an actor,
That paces and worries about his time on stage,
And then is silent: it is a story
Told by a fool, full of noise and anger,
Amounting to nothing.

Enter Messenger.

79
MESSENGER:
Respected sir,
I am supposed to report what I saw,
But don't know how to do it.
MACBETH:
Just say it, sir.
MESSENGER:
As I stood guard on the hill,
I looked towards Birnam, and suddenly, it seemed,
The forest started to move.

MACBETH:

Liar!

MESSENGER:

Listen to me and look for yourself.

Within three miles you can see it coming;

... moving forest!

MACBETH:

If your words are a lie,

Upon the next tree you'll hang alive,

Until hunger takes you: if your words holds truth,

I won't mind if you do that instead to me.—

I lose my determination; and start

To doubt the deceit of the devil,

Which lies like truth. "Fear not, until Birnam forest

Comes to Dunsinane;" and now a forest

Is heading toward Dunsinane.

—Get ready, get ready, and let's go!—

If what he claims appears to be true,

There's no point in running or staying here.

I'm beginning to be tired of the sun,

And wish everything in the world could end now.—

Ring the alarm bell!—Blow, wind! Let chaos come!

At least we'll die with our armor on our back.

They all exit.

SCENE VI. THE SAME. A PLAIN BEFORE THE CASTLE.

80 *[Enter, with drums and flags, Malcolm, old Siward, Macduff, and their Army, holding branches.]*

MALCOLM:
Now we're close enough. Drop your branches,
And show yourselves as you truly are.
—You, respectable uncle,
Alongside my cousin, your truly noble son,
Will lead our first battle: worthy Macduff and I
Will take care of what else remains to be done,
Following our plans.

SIWARD:
Good luck to you.—
If we only meet the tyrant's forces tonight,
Let us lose, if we can't fight.

MACDUFF:
Let all our trumpets sound; give them full strength,

The noisy signals of bloodshed and death.

They all exit.

SCENE VII. THE SAME. ANOTHER PART OF THE FIELD

 [ALARMS SOUND. MACBETH ENTERS.]

MACBETH:
I'm bound and I can't escape, but
I must fight this out. Why should I fear a man
Who was born from a woman?
One who is not I am to fear,
but that's impossible.

Enter Young Siward.

YOUNG SIWARD:
What is your name?
MACBETH:
You'd be scared to hear it.
YOUNG SIWARD:
No--unless you name yourself something more terrifying
than any demon in hell.
MACBETH:
My name's Macbeth.

YOUNG SIWARD:

Even the devil couldn't say a name

More hateful to my hearing.

MACBETH:

Nor more frightening.

YOUNG SIWARD:

Despised ruler: with my sword,

I'll prove the lie you're speaking.

They fight, and young Siward is killed.

MACBETH:

You were born of a woman.

I laugh at swords, mock weapons,

Wielded by a man born of a woman.

He exits. Alarms sound. Macduff enters.

MACDUFF:

The noise is this way. Tyrant, show yourself!

If you're killed and not by my hand,

The ghosts of my wife and children will haunt me endlessly.

I can't attack mere soldiers...

It's either you, Macbeth,

Or my sword goes back in its sheath, still clean. There you should be.

Let me find him, Fortune!

And I ask for nothing more.

He exits. Alarms sound. Malcolm and old Siward enter.

SIWARD:

This way, my lord; the castle has surrendered quietly:

The dictator's forces are fighting on both sides;

The lords are courageous in the battle,

The day itself appears to be ours for winning

And there is little left to do.

MALCOLM:

We have encountered enemies

That strike alongside us.
SIWARD:
Enter, sir, into the castle.

They exit. Alarms continue to sound.

SCENE VIII. THE SAME. ANOTHER PART OF THE FIELD.

 [ENTER MACBETH.]

MACBETH:
Why should I act like the Romans,
and kill myself? As I see others survive,
their wounds seem to heal faster.

Enter Macduff.

MACDUFF:
Turn, evil one!

MACBETH:
I've avoided all men, especially you.
However, step back--
my soul is already overloaded with your family's blood.

MACDUFF:
I have no words;
my actions speak for me:
you are more wicked than can be described!

They fight.

MACBETH:
You waste effort:
as easily as you can mark the untouched air
with your sharp sword.
I have a protected life,
which won't end by the hand of someone born of a woman.
MACDUFF:
Forget your false protection!
Let the angel who has served you tell you this:
I, Macduff, was unnaturally cut from my mother's womb!
MACBETH:
Damn the messenger who tells me this,
it has taken my courage away!
And I won't trust those deceptive witches
who manipulate us anymore;
who keep the promise,
but then break it when it comes to our hope!
I won't fight you.
MACDUFF:
Then surrender, coward,
and live on to be the show and talk of the time.
Just like our rarest creatures,
you will be put on display and carry the label:
"Tyrant."
MACBETH:
I won't surrender,
I refuse to bow before young Malcolm's feet.
And to be scorned by the common people.
Even if Birnam forest has arrived at Dunsinane,
and you, who wasn't born from a woman,
stand against me, I'll still fight till the end.
I raise my shield: let's go, Macduff;
and cursed be the one who first cries, "Hold, enough!"

84

They exit fighting, followed by alarm bells. Everyone retreats. Enter Malcolm, old Siward, Ross, Thanes and Soldiers, with drums and flags.

MALCOLM:

I wish the friends we're missing had safely arrived.

SIWARD:

Some had to go; but looking at those here,

I'd say this great day comes at a small cost.

MALCOLM:

We are still missing Macduff and your brave son.

ROSS:

My lord, you son fulfilled his duty as a soldier:

he lived until he was a man.

As soon as his bravery was proven on the battlefield,

he died as a true man.

SIWARD:

Then he is dead?

FLEANCE:

He is, and was removed from the battlefield.

Your grief shouldn't be measured by his worth,

since that would be never-ending.

SIWARD:

Did he get his injuries on the front lines?

ROSS:

Yes, right at the forefront.

SIWARD:

Well, then he was indeed God's soldier! If I had as many sons as hairs,

I would pray for them all to meet such an honourable end.

MALCOLM:

He deserves more sorrow, which I'll provide.

SIWARD:

No more sorrow for him.

They say he fought well and settled his debts,

So, may God be with him!—

But look, here comes some better news.

Enter Macduff with Macbeth's head.

MACDUFF:

Greetings, King, for that is what you are.

Look, here is the head of the usurper: we are free at last!

I see you're ready with an important message

That can bring peace to our country.

I ask all to join in saying:

Hail, King of Scotland!

ALL:

Hail, King of Scotland!

Celebration.

.

MALCOLM:

We shall not spend a large expense of time

Before we fix everything.

My thanes and kinsmen,

Henceforth be earls, the first that ever Scotland ever had.

Let's bring home our friends,

Who fled Macbeth's rule and

Macbeth's fiend-like queen,

Who took her life.

By the grace of Grace,

We will perform in measure, time, and place.

So thanks to all at once, and to each one,

Whom we invite to see us crowned at Scone.

Cheerful celebration. They exit.

www.ingramcontent.com/pod-product-compliance
Lightning Source LLC
Chambersburg PA
CBHW022011150726
47990CB00002B/613